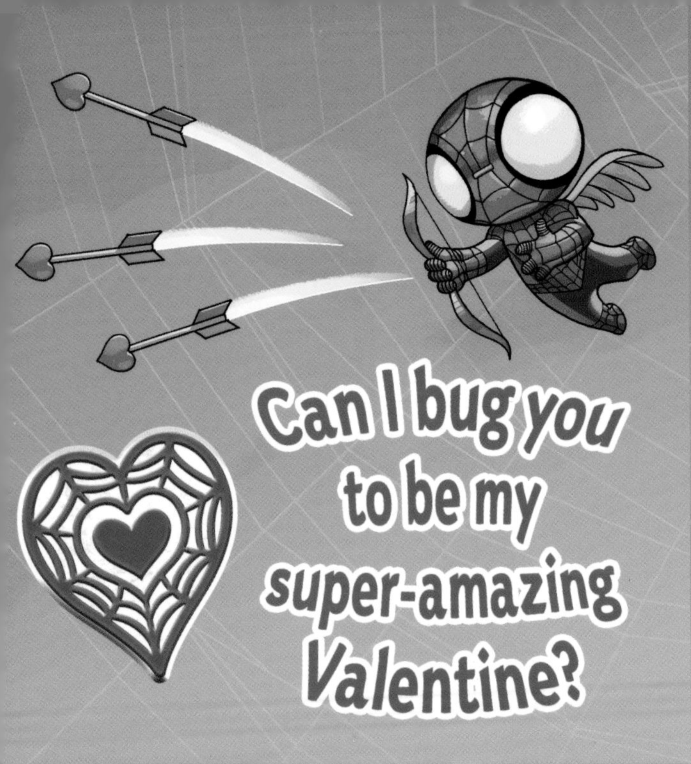
Can I bug you
to be my
super-amazing
Valentine?
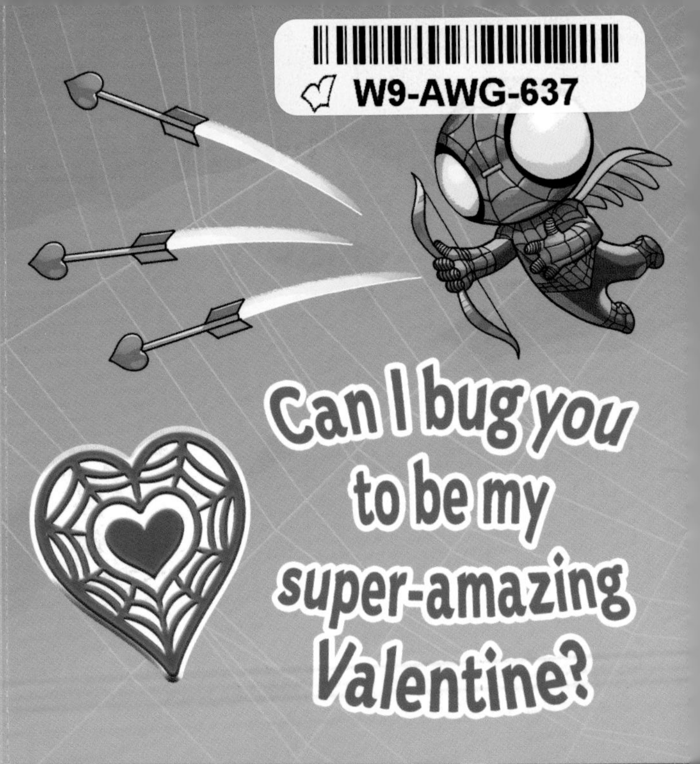
Can I bug you
to be my
super-amazing
Valentine?

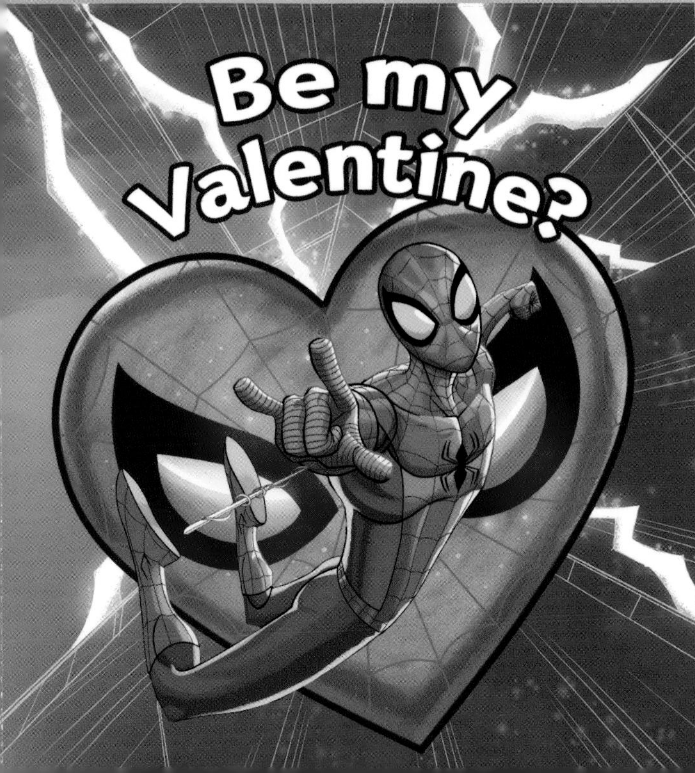
Be my
Valentine?
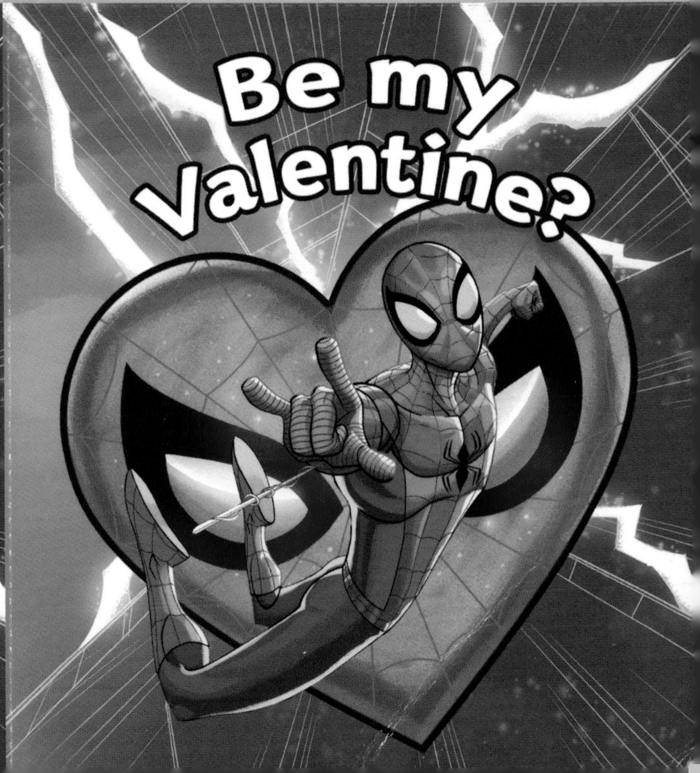
Be my
Valentine?

Happy Valentine's Day!

To: _____

From: _____

Happy Valentine's Day!

To: _____

From: _____

Happy Valentine's Day!

To: _____

From: _____

Happy Valentine's Day!

To: _____

From: _____

MARVEL

SPIDER-MAN

Love Bug

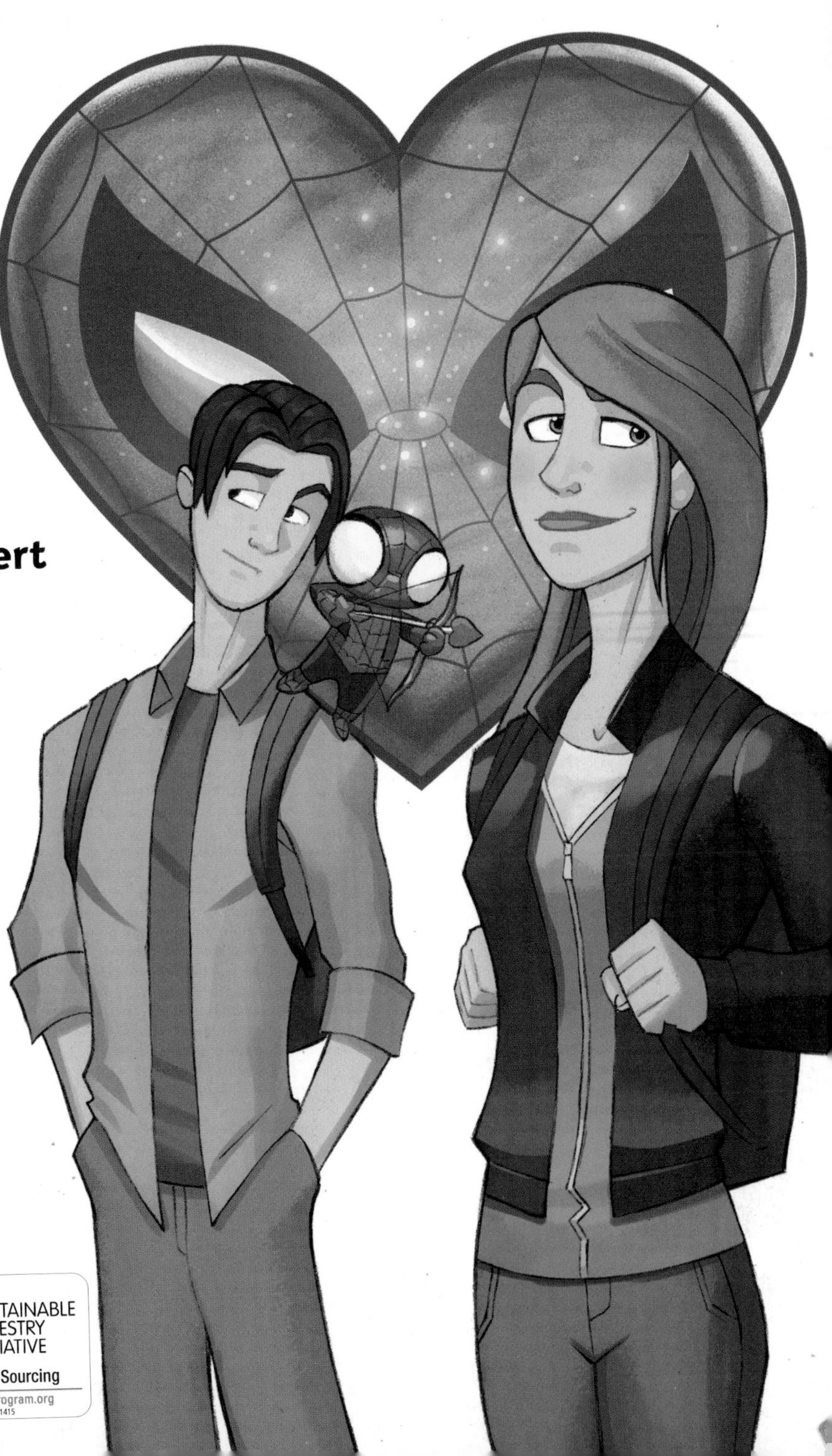

Vritten by **Thomas Macri**

lustrated by **Christian Colbert** and **Matt Milla**

3ased on the Marvel comic book series *Spider-Man*

MARVEL
narvelkids.com

Manufactured in the United States of America
First Edition, December 2015
10 9 8 7 6 5 4 3 2 1
ISBN 978-1-4847-3128-4
FAC-029261-15296
Library of Congress Control Number: 2015935075

SUSTAINABLE FORESTRY INITIATIVE
Certified Sourcing
www.sfiprogram.org
SFI-01415

On his way to school, Peter felt a strange tingling. But it was not an allergic reaction to his peanut-butter-and-jelly sandwich. It was his spidey-sense! Peter wasn't just a high school student.

He was also the famous Super Hero Spider-Man.

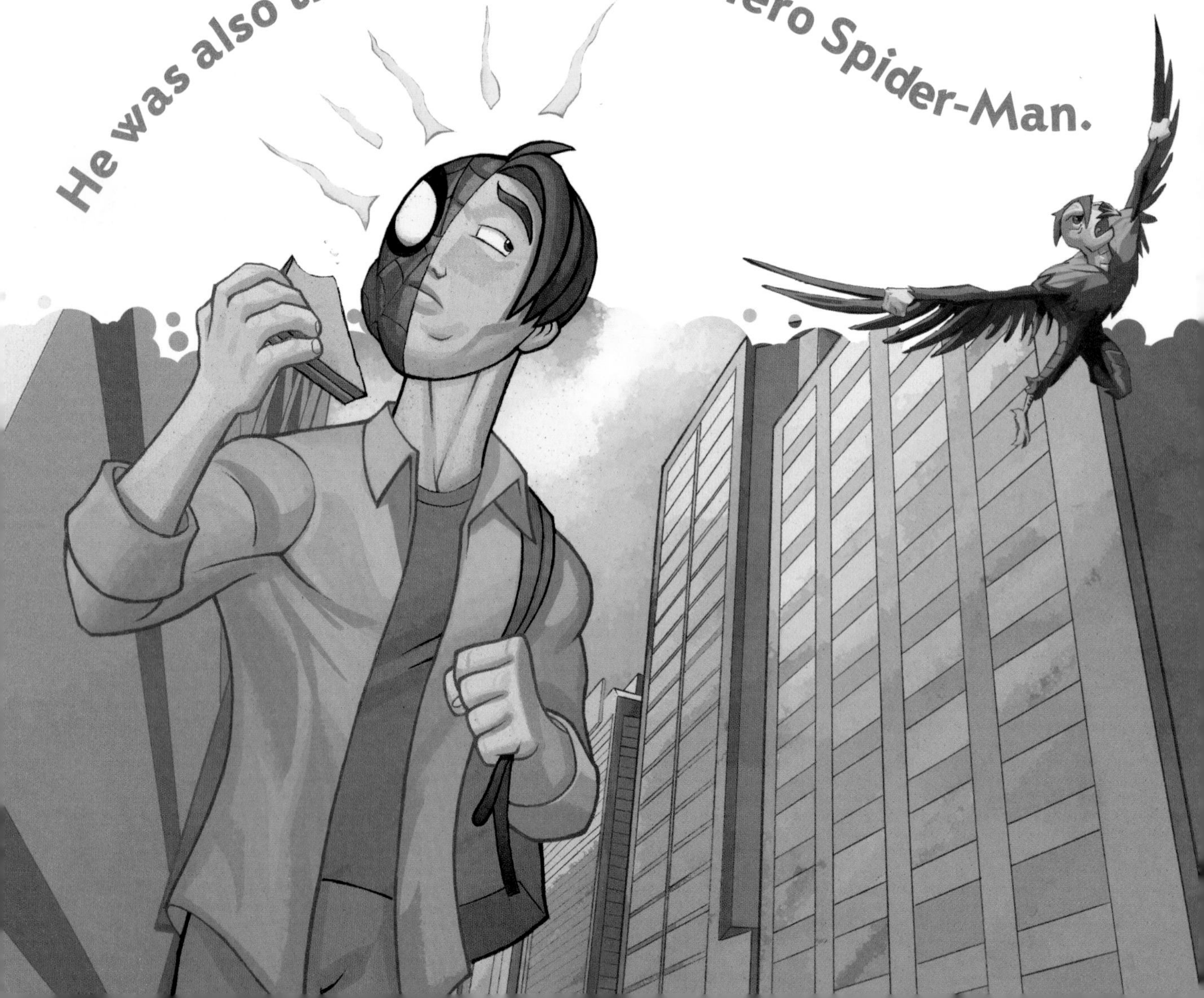

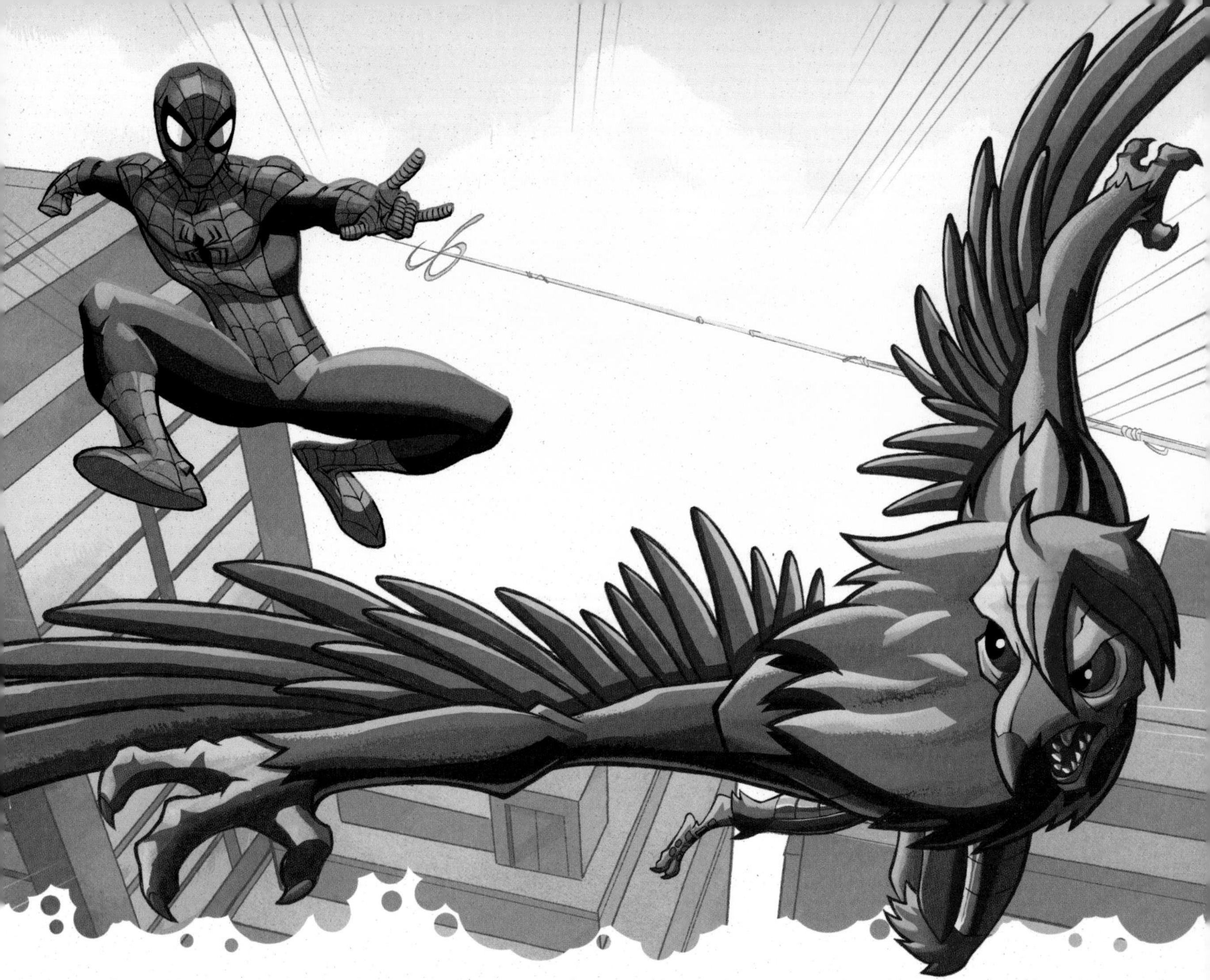

After a quick costume change, Spider-Man chased the villain he etected in the sky. It was Vulture!

"Hey, birdbrain! Shouldn't you have flown south for the winter?" Spider-Man said.

"Spider-Man! Out of my way!" Vulture yelled.

Oh, boy. I am going to be really late to school, thought Peter.

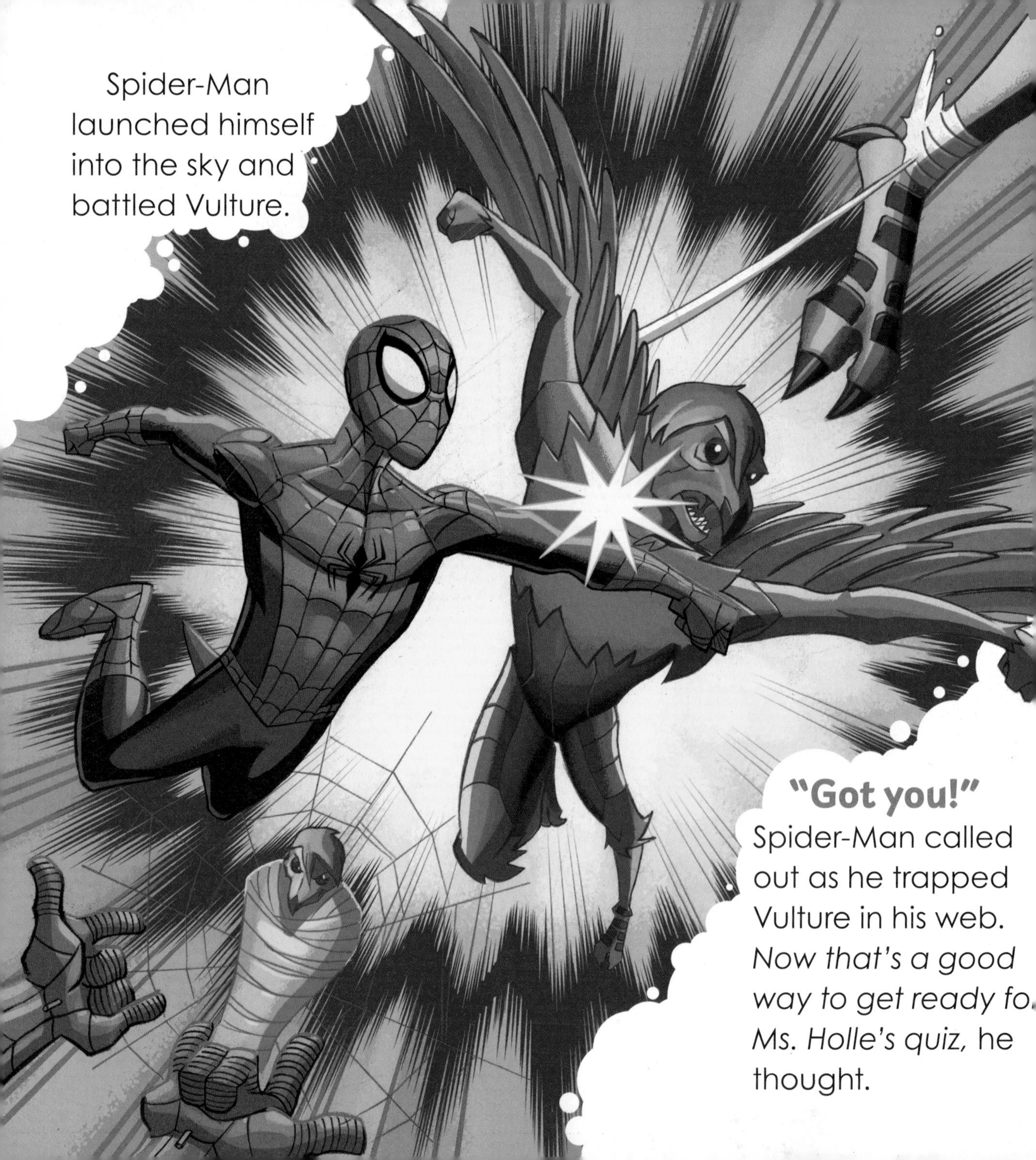

Spider-Man launched himself into the sky and battled Vulture.

"Got you!" Spider-Man called out as he trapped Vulture in his web. *Now that's a good way to get ready fo Ms. Holle's quiz,* he thought.

"I can't miss first period," Peter mumbled to himself. That's the only class I have with Mary Jane!" Then he wung off to school just as the police arrived.

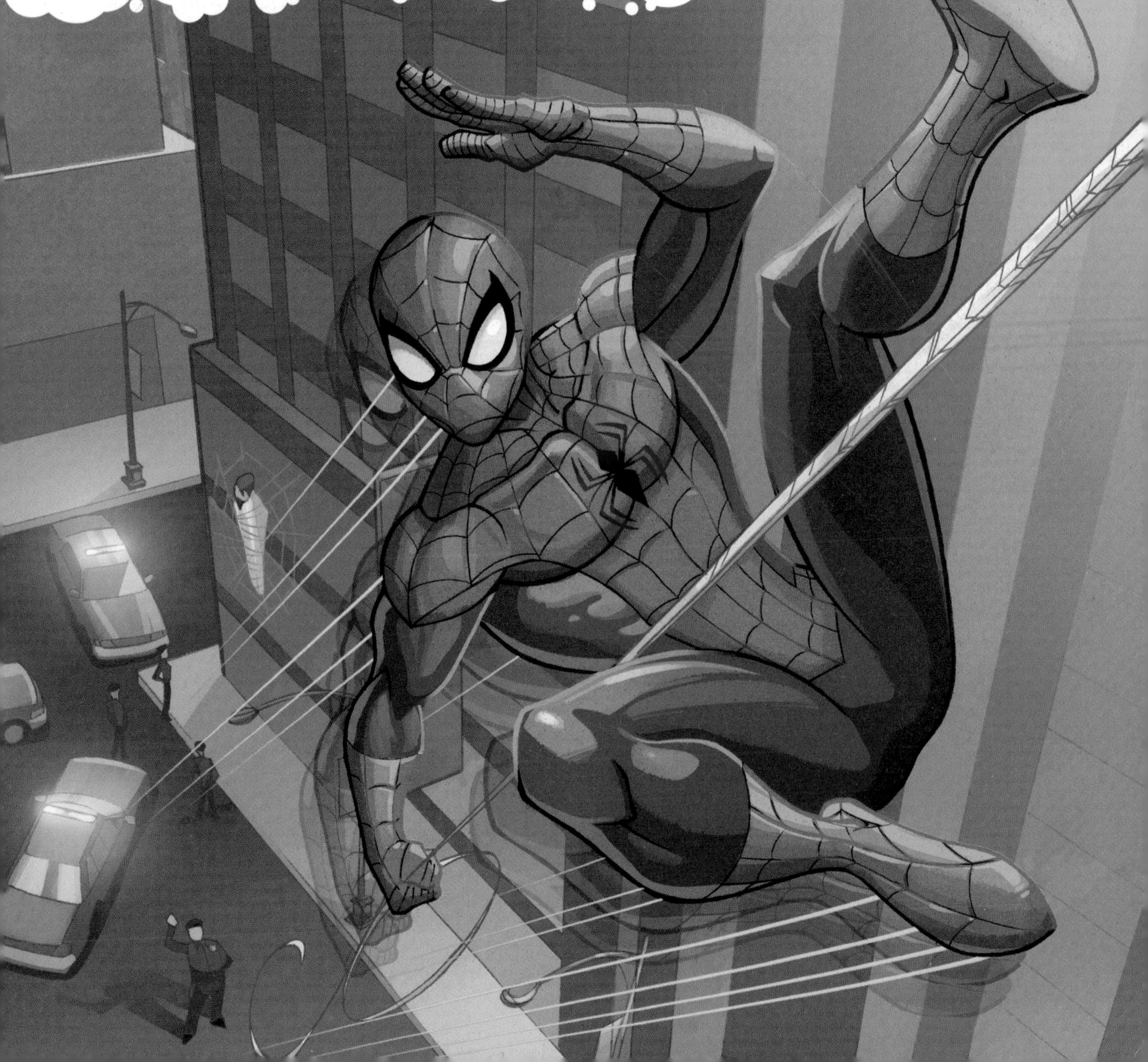

Peter arrived, still dressed as Spider-Man, just as Ms. Holle turned to write on the chalkboard. He pulled on his street clothes and slipped into his seat unnoticed.

"Is everyone ready for the quiz? Oh, Peter! I didn't realize you were here. I marked you as absent," Ms. Holle said, surprised.

Peter smiled.

That was a close one!

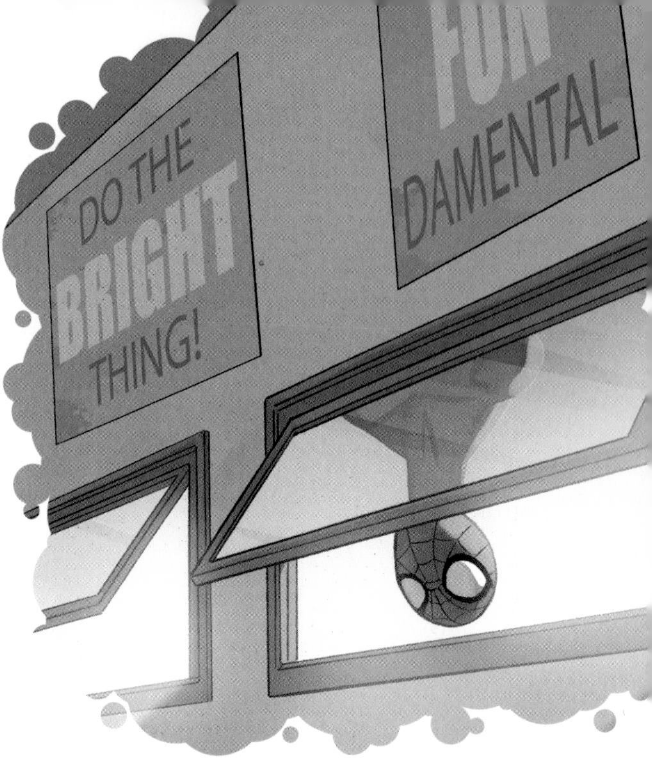
DO THE BRIGHT THING!
DAMENTAL

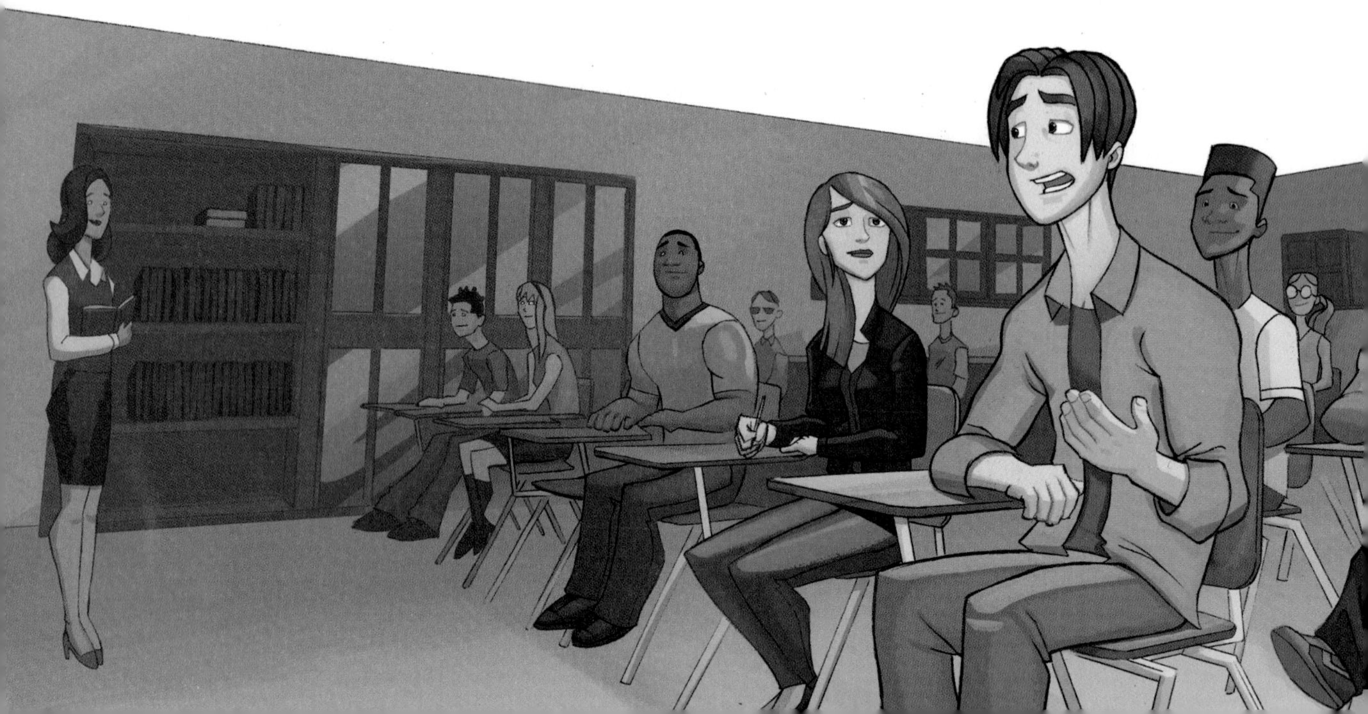

Peter loved science more than anything, except Mary Jane. Whether hitting a home run, cheering at a pep rally, or taking the lead in a school musical,

she was always a star.

And Peter couldn't help daydreaming when she was around—even during a quiz. . . .

"Peter!" Ms. Holle snapped. "Time is almost up!"
He pulled himself together and finished the quiz.

"Hey, tiger!"

Mary Jane said to Peter after class. Tiger was her special nickname for him, and it always made Peter blush and smile.

"Listen, there's a free play in Central Park during lunch. I know you wouldn't usually be interested, but this one's about a scientist who is scared of his own shadow!" Mary Jane said.

"I'm not scared. Do I look scared?" Peter said quickly.

"Um, no," Mary Jane said, giggling. "But you do love science."

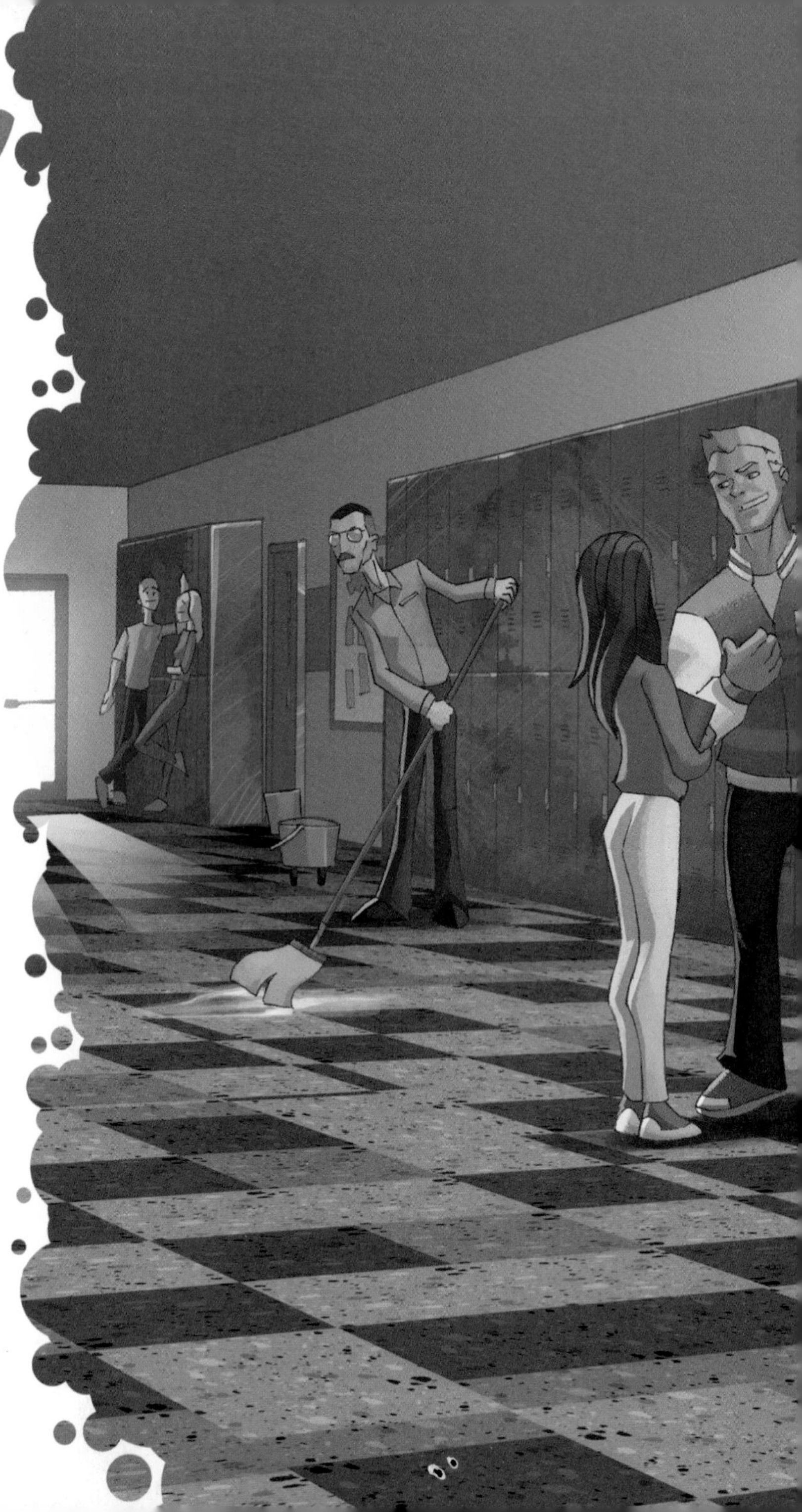

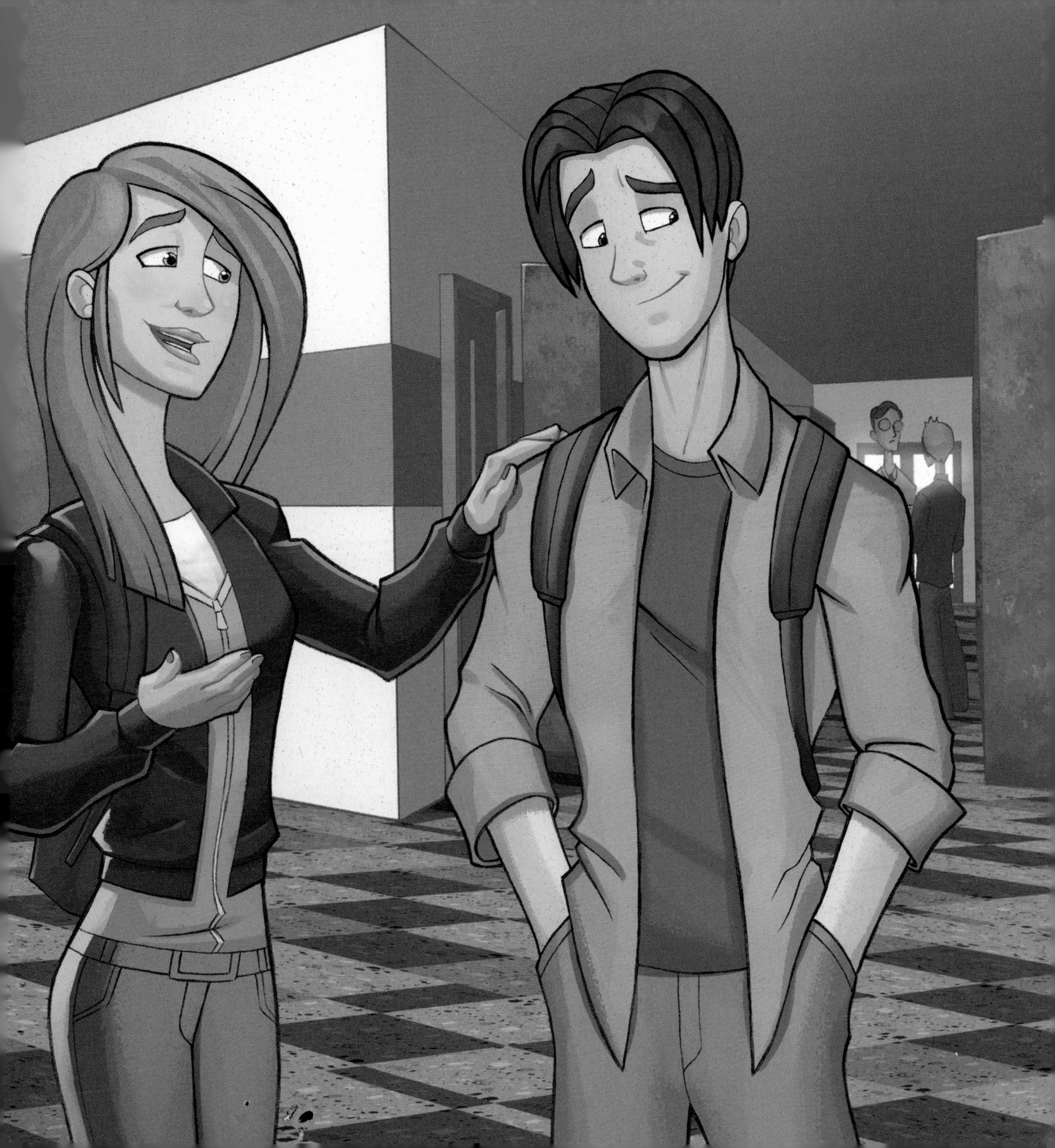

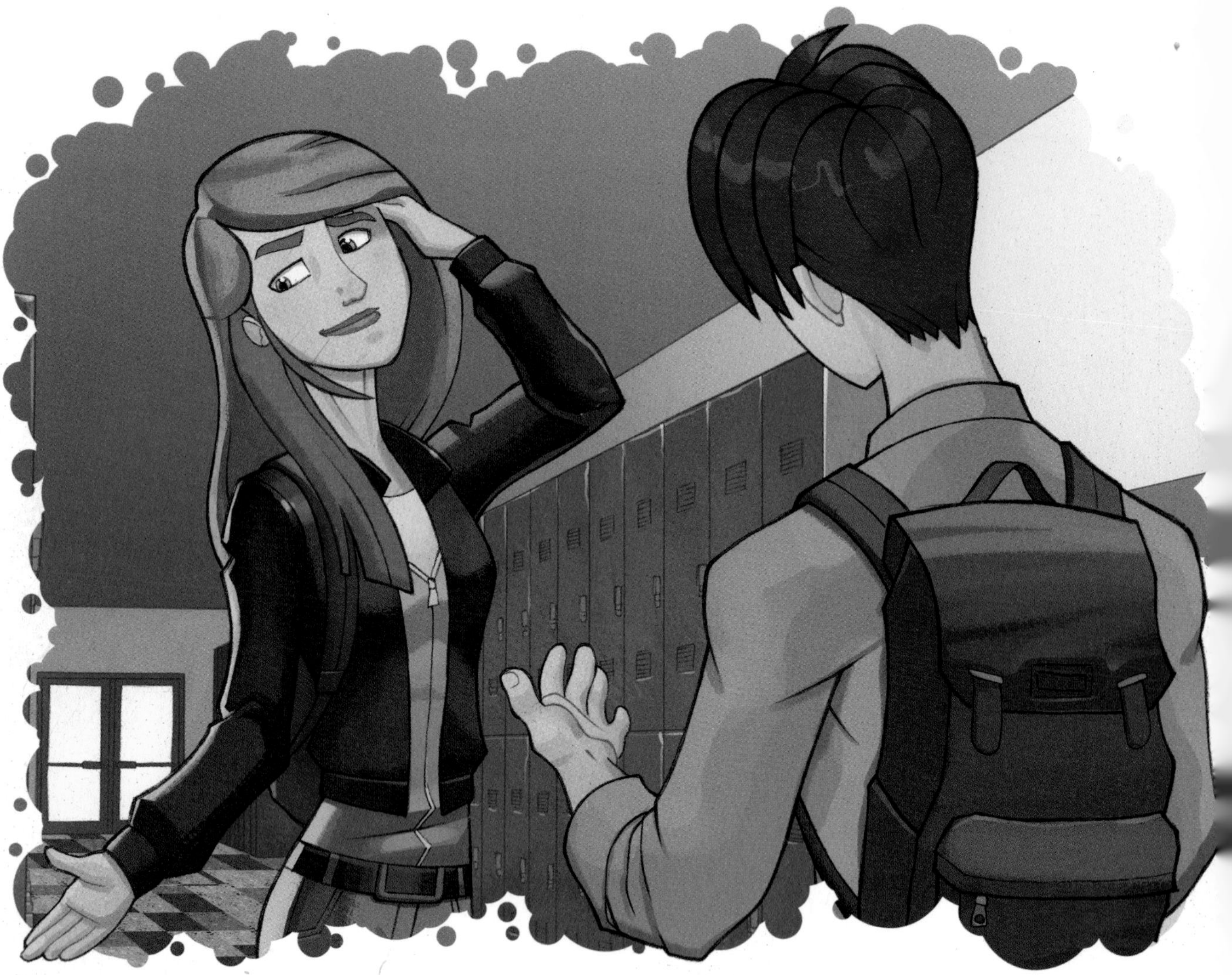

Peter couldn't believe it. Was Mary Jane really asking him out on a sort-of-maybe date?

"Yes, definitely!" Peter shouted. Then, not wanting to sound too eager, he added, "I mean—*ahem*—that sounds great."

"Good! Let's head over there together so we can grab a slice of pizza before the play," Mary Jane said.

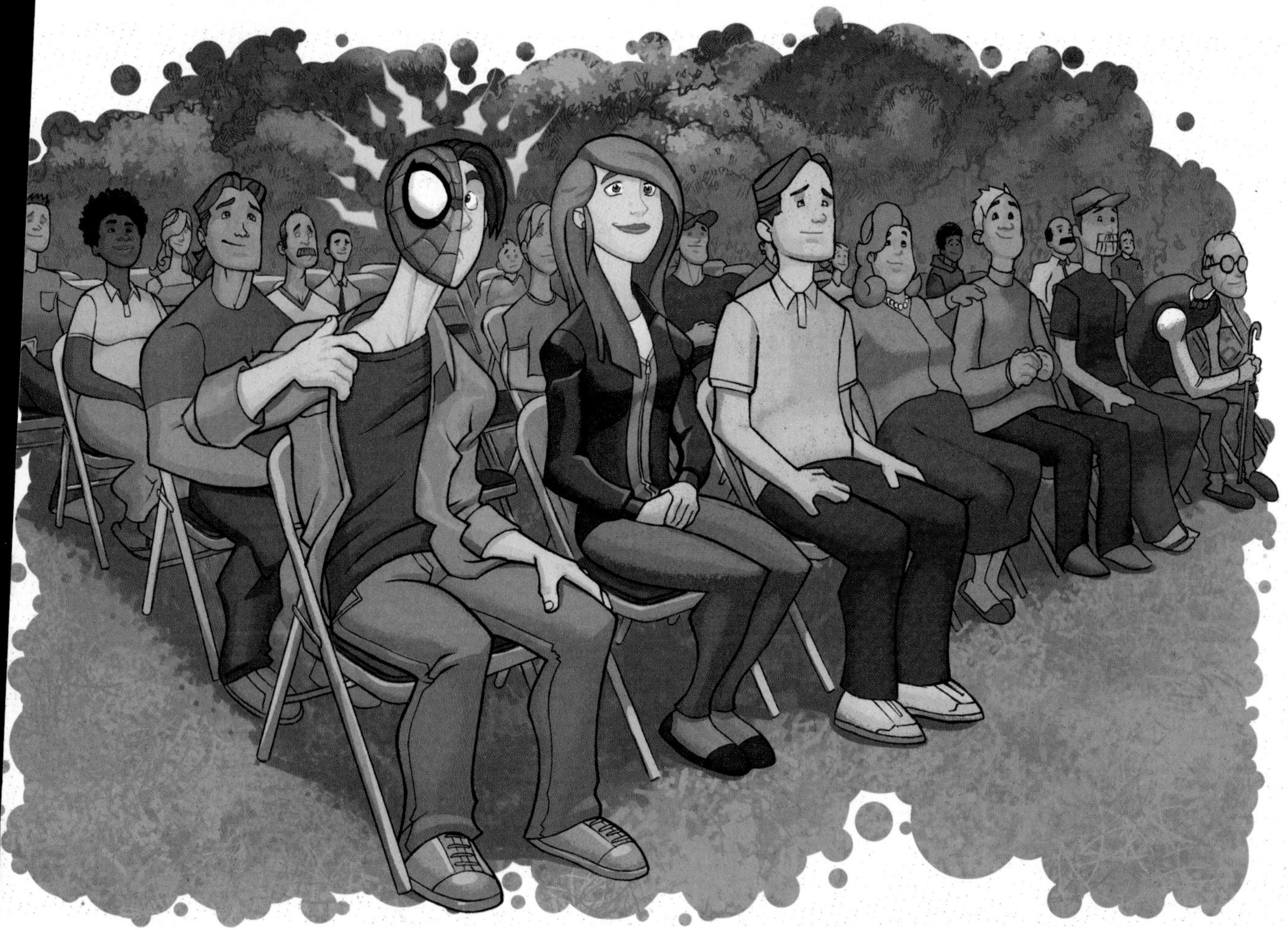

They finally found their seats. Everyone was ready for a good show.

"I'm really excited!" MJ said.

"I've wanted to see this play for forever!"

Peter started to smile, but he once again felt that familiar tingling. *It's only the first act of the play!* he thought. *Something's wrong, and I'm not sure it can wait until intermission.*

"I'll be right back," he whispered to MJ before disappearing. He hoped she wasn't annoyed.

A moment later Peter came out as Spider-Man!

"I think I've done as many costume changes as a lead actor!" Spider-Man grumbled. He searched the park to see what had set off his spider-sense. Soon he found the answer—Rhino!

"Look who escaped from the Central Park Zoo!" Spider-Man joked.

Rhino did not look happy to see Spider-Man! He roared and charged at the hero.

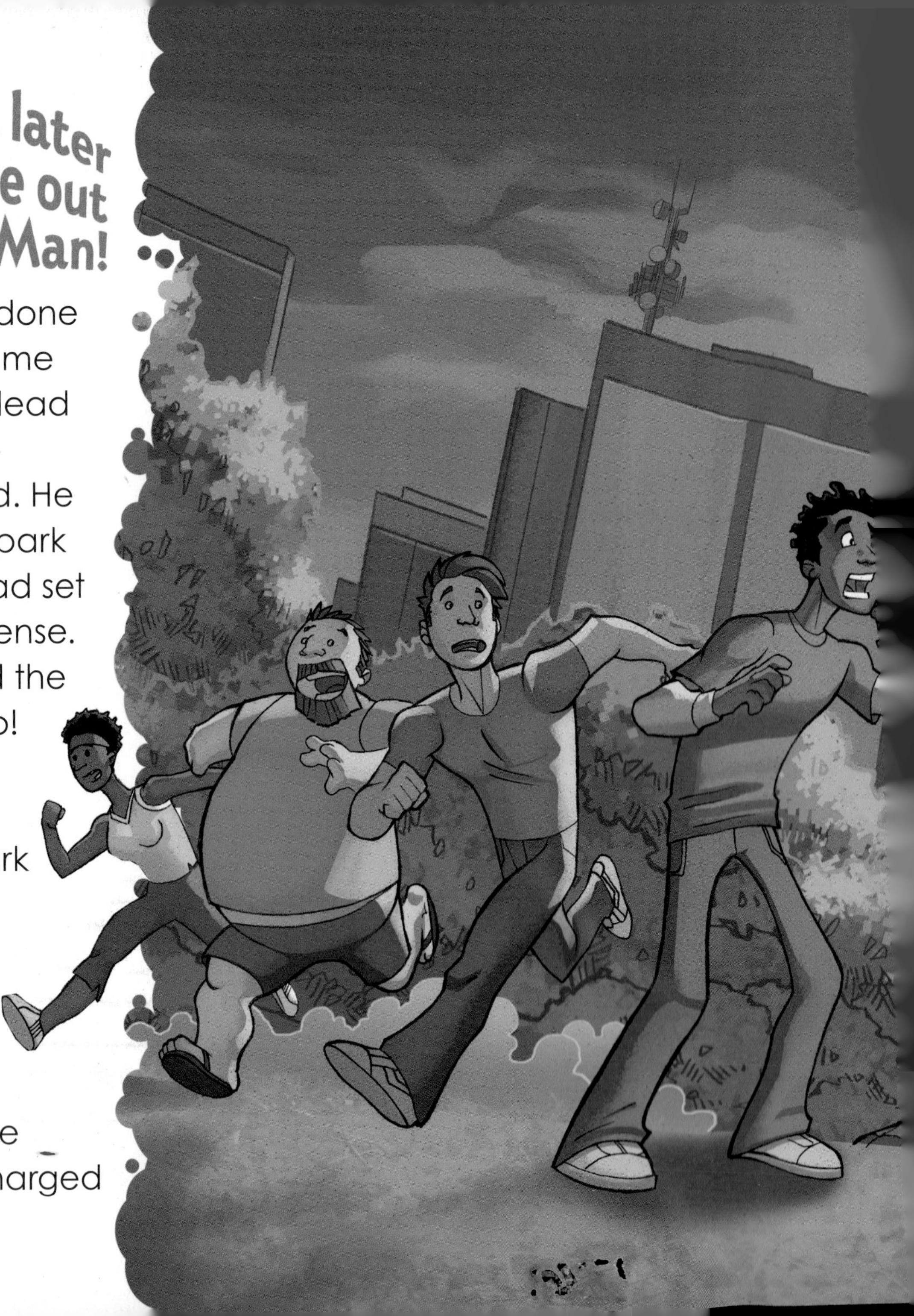

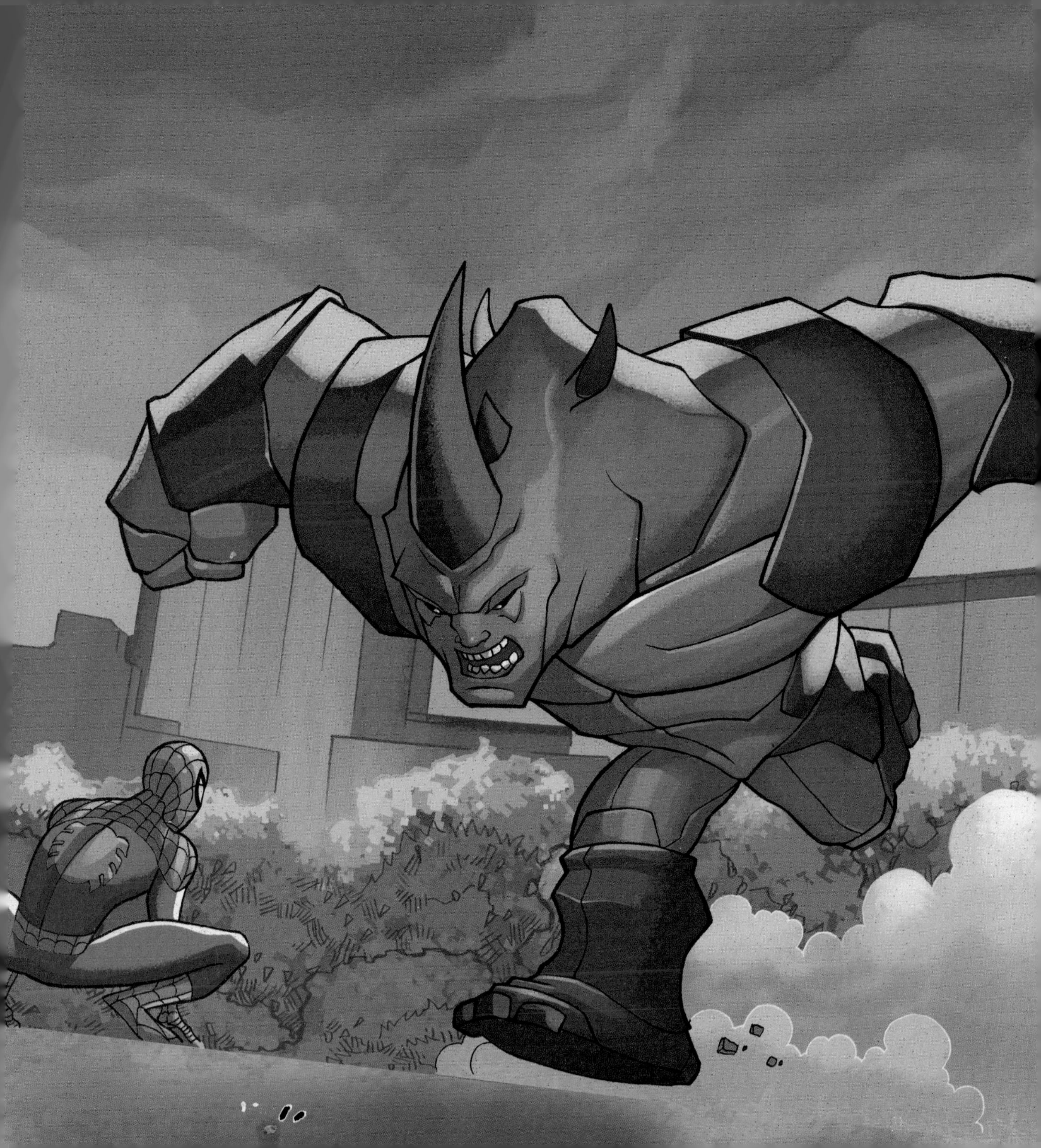

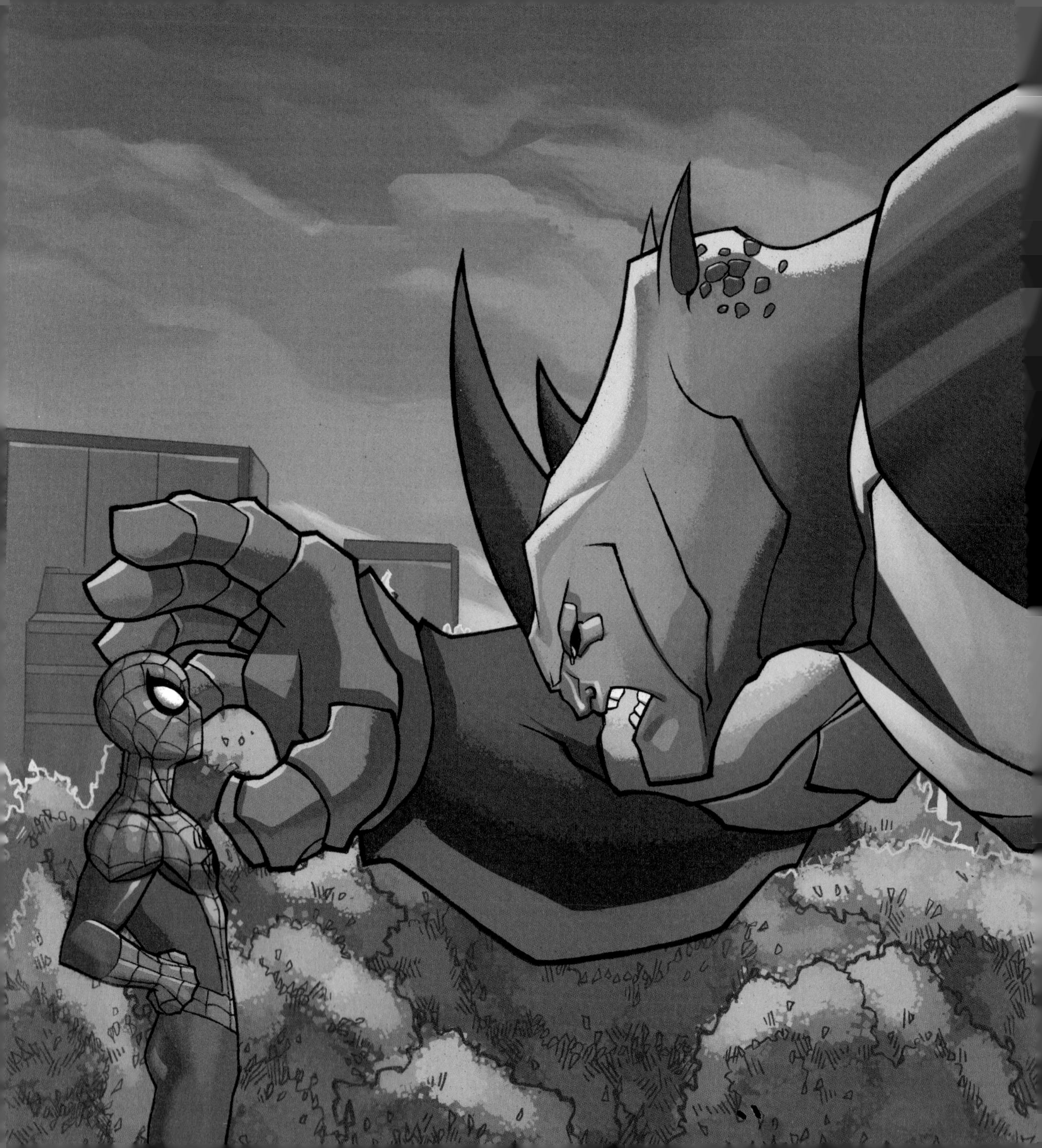

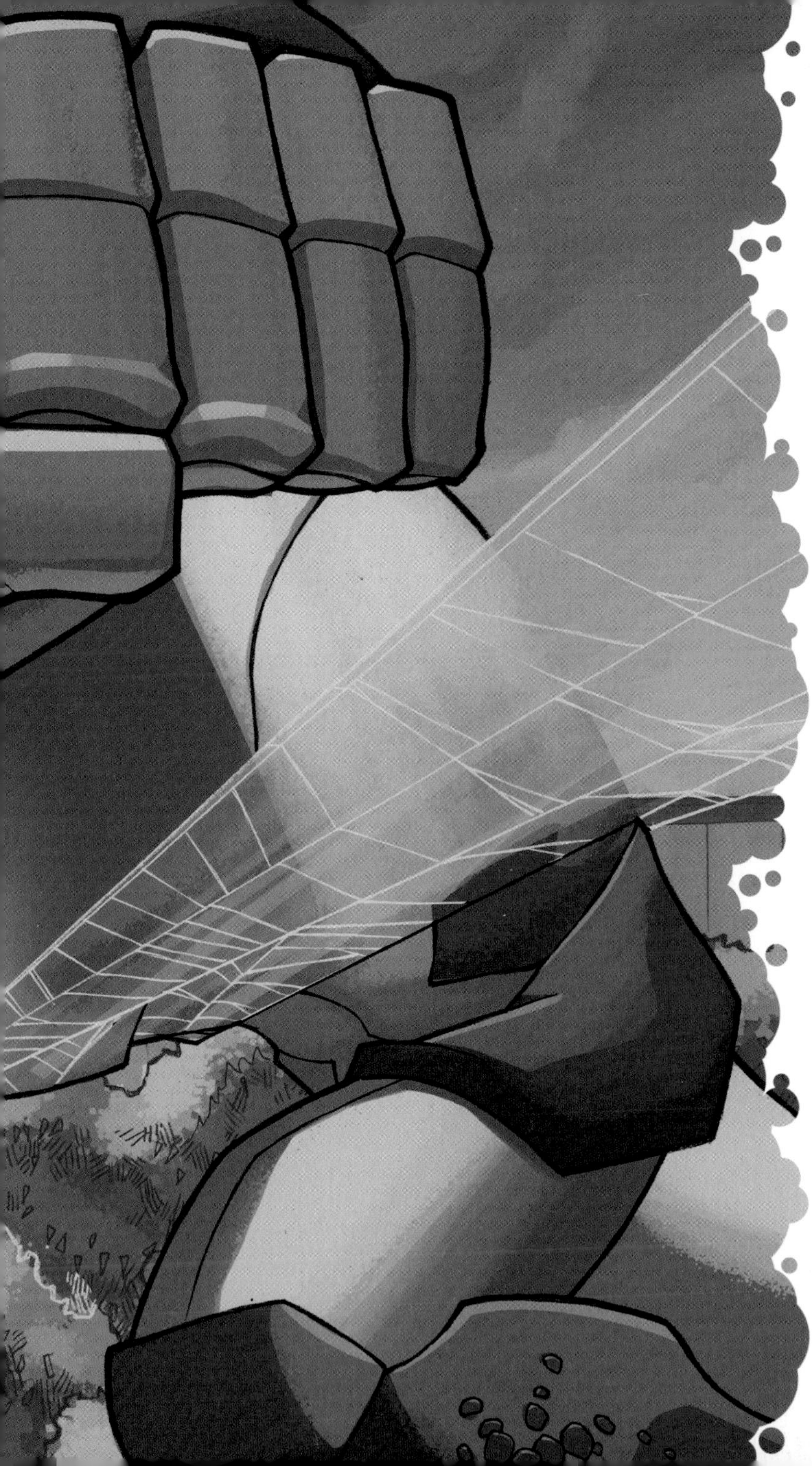

Yikes! *There are too many bystanders to get out of the way in time!* Spider-Man thought. **Swiftly, Spidey made his webbing into a giant slingshot.**

"Ha! You don't think I can break your little webs? I'm huge!" Rhino laughed as he picked up his speed.

"Your head is as thick as your skin!" Spider-Man said, taunting him.

Rhino stampeded right into Spider-Man's webbing. As soon as he made contact with the web, he was shot into the distance . . .

. . . and became a tiny speck in the sky.

Peter ran back to the play after a quick change.

"Peter, you're sweating! What happened?" MJ asked.

"It—it got really hot. I had to step out," Peter replied nervously.

"Well, you certainly missed a show!"

"I know. . . . I'm so sorry, MJ." Peter felt bad. That was not how he had wanted his date with MJ to go. She deserved better!

"No, I mean Spider-Man was here! There was so much commotion, the play stopped. It turned out it was Spider-Man battling Rhino!" MJ told Peter.

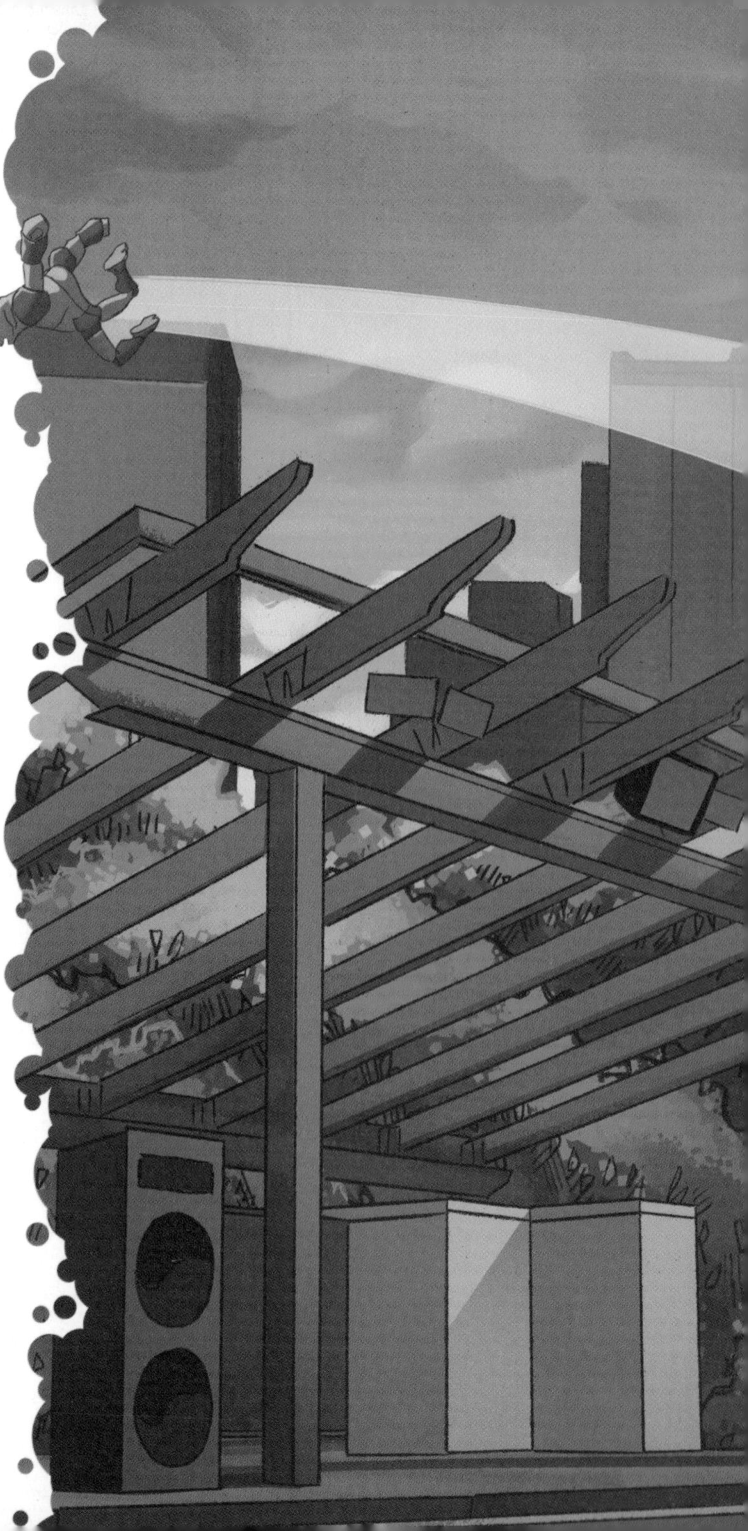

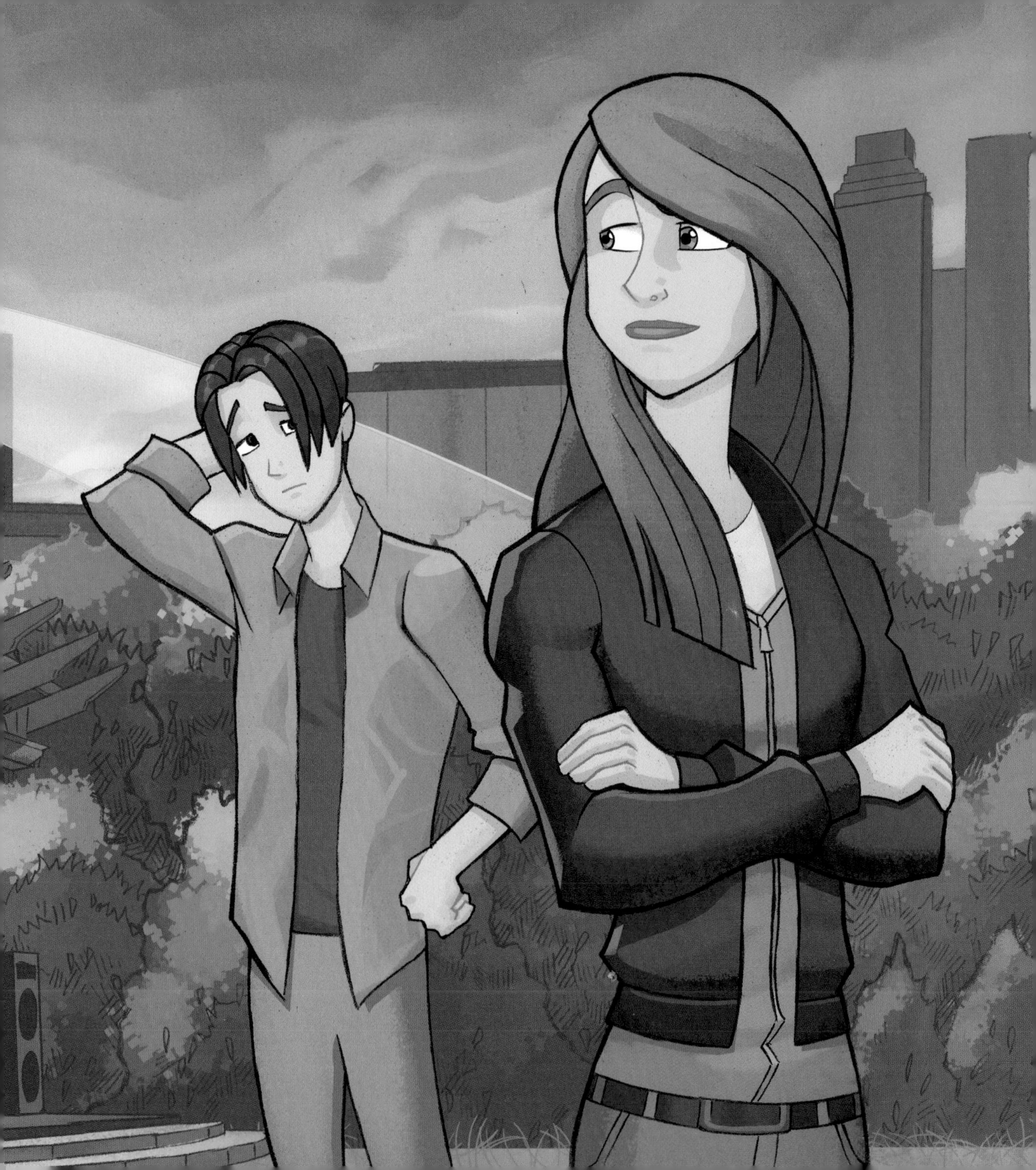

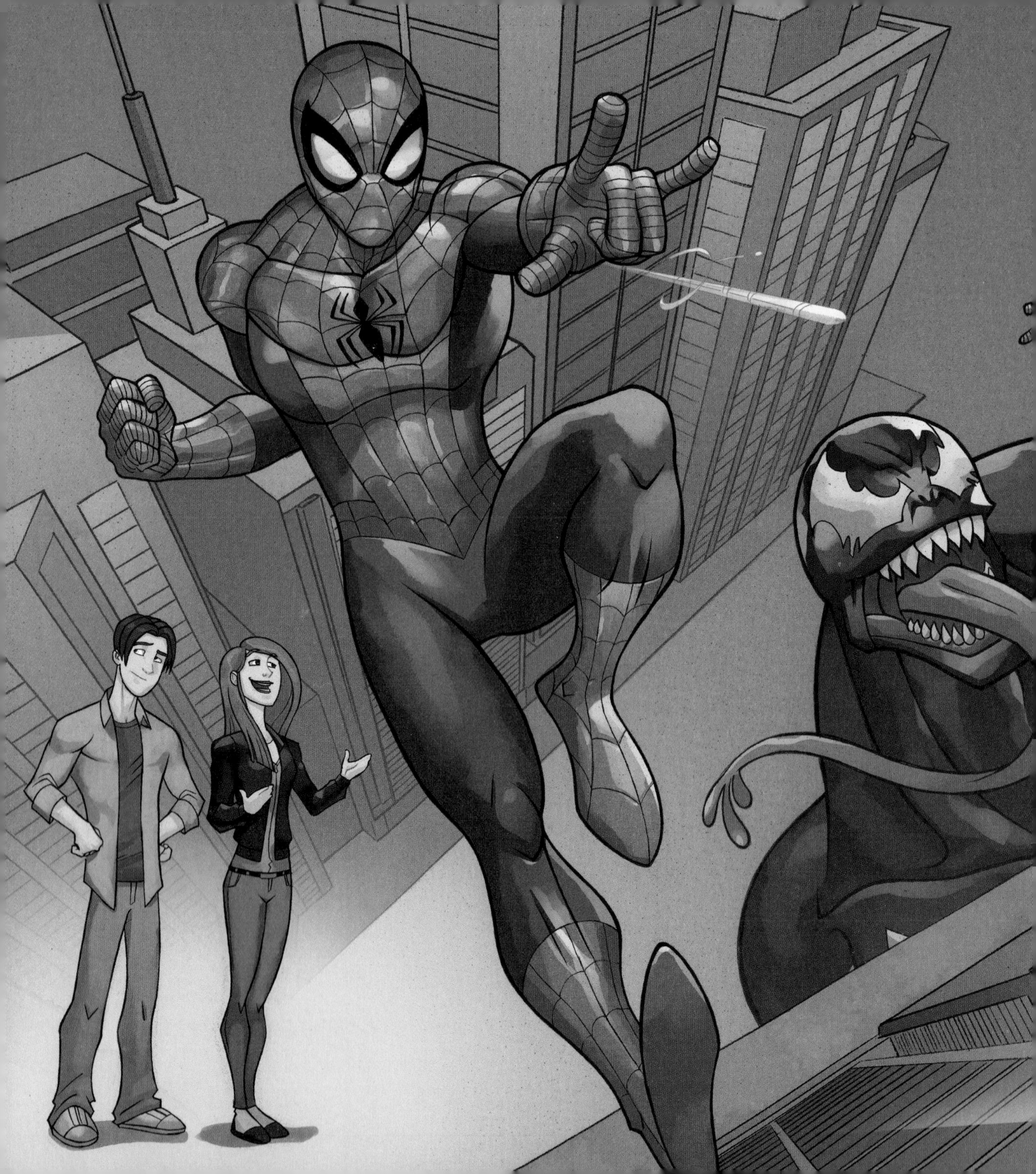

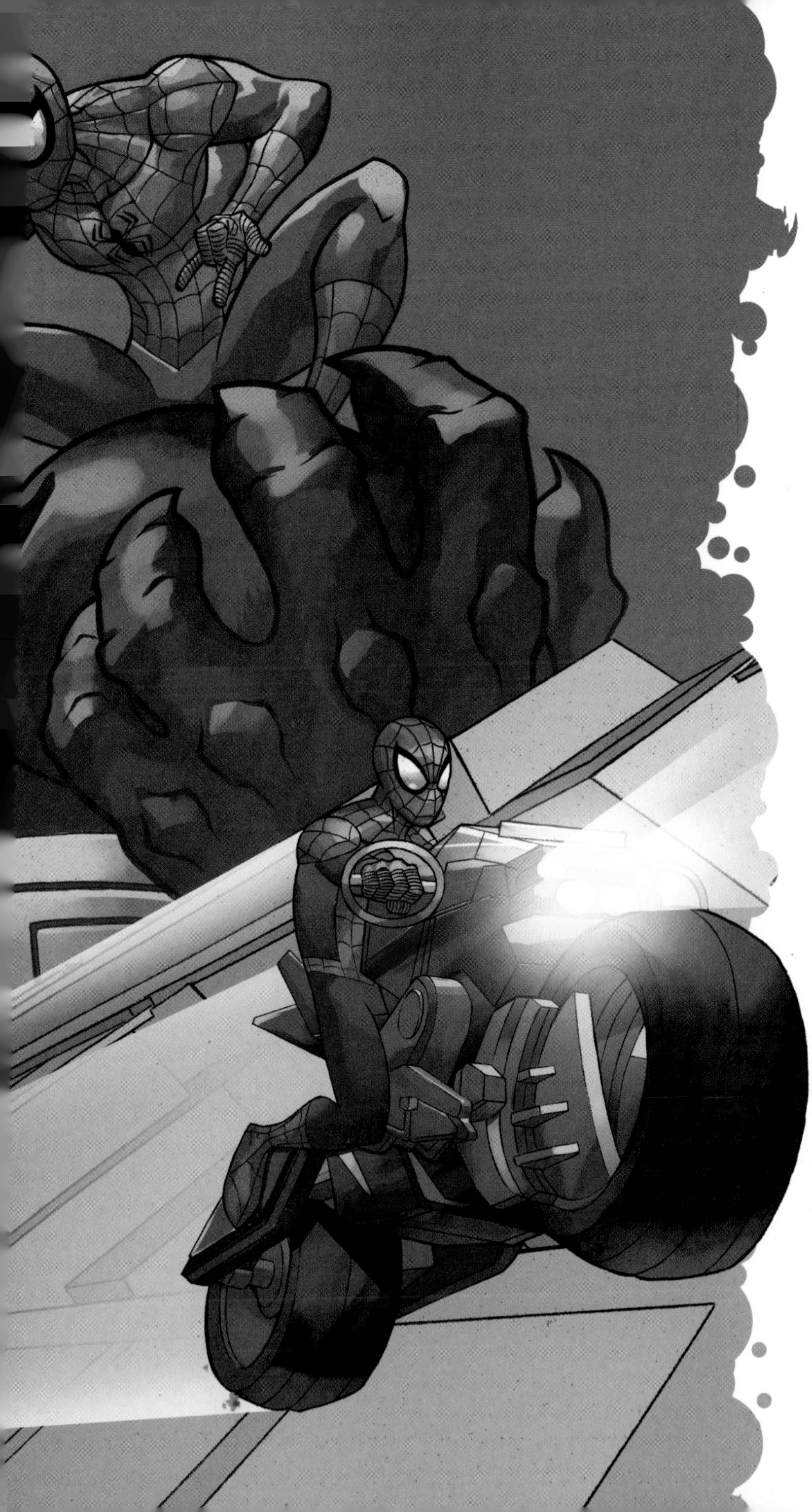

"Really? You saw that?" Peter asked, shocked.

"Totally! He was amazing," MJ gushed.

"Oh, he's not bad." Peter tried to play it cool.

"'Not bad'? Spidey's my hero! He can swing from rooftop to rooftop. He fights villains and always saves the day. . . . He even has a bike that climbs walls!"

Peter suddenly felt good inside. Maybe he had actually impressed MJ. . . . But then he remembered no one knew Peter Parker was Spider-Man.

Mary-Jane saw that Peter looked sad. "Don't worry. You're not so bad yourself. . . . You just have really bad luck with timing," she said with a laugh.

"Tell me about it," Peter replied, shaking his head.

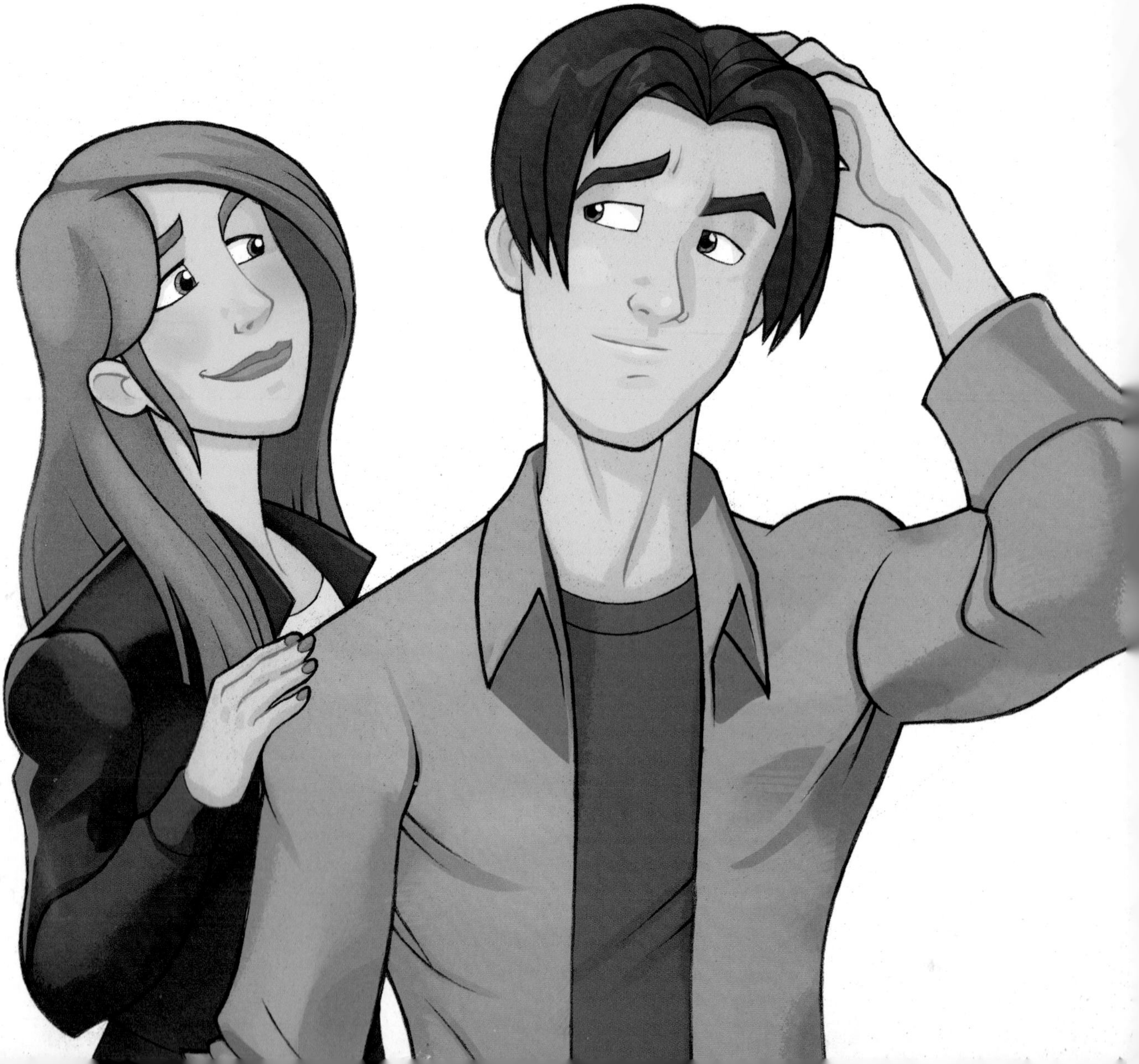

Happy Valentine's Day!

To: _____

From: _____

Happy Valentine's Day!

To: _____

From: _____

Happy Valentine's Day!

To: _____

From: _____

Happy Valentine's Day!

To: _____

From: _____

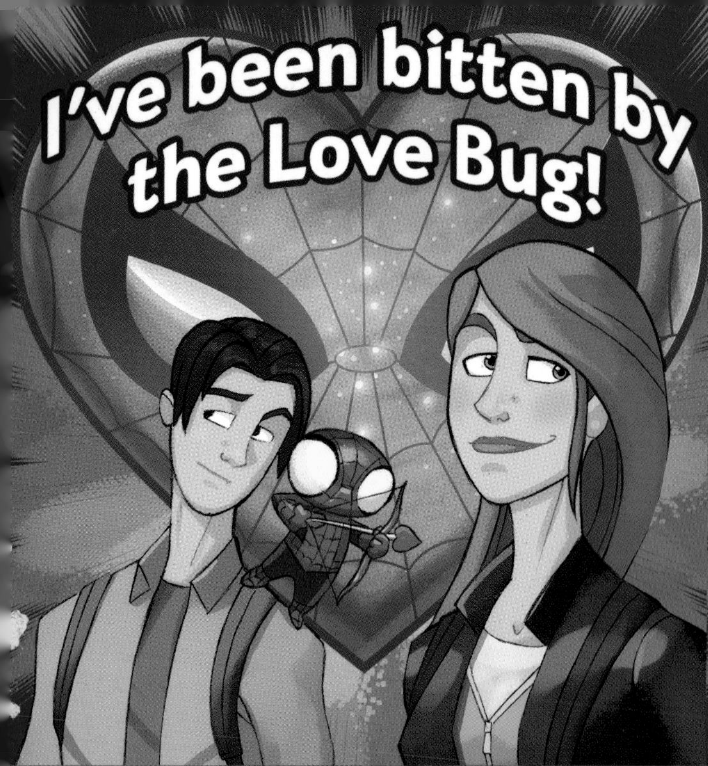
I've been bitten by
the Love Bug!

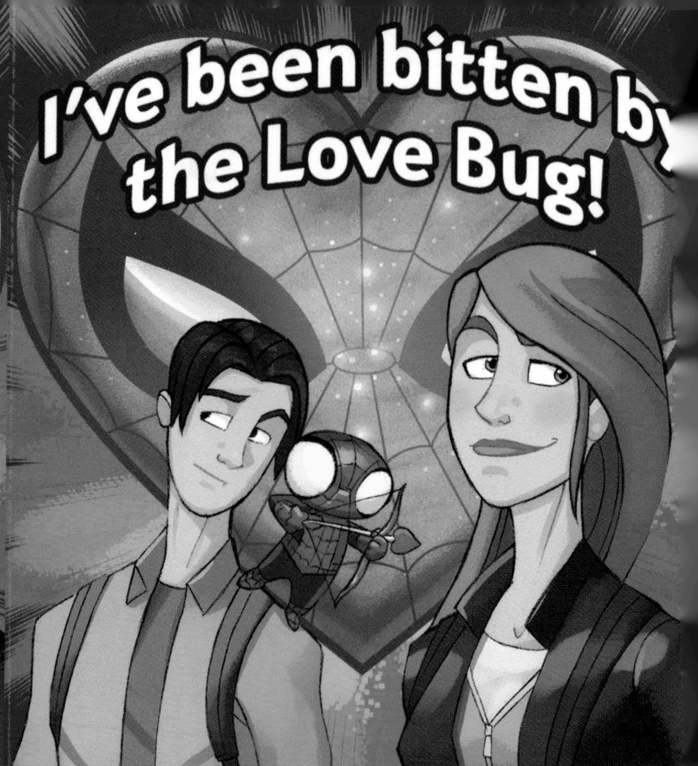
I've been bitten b
the Love Bug!

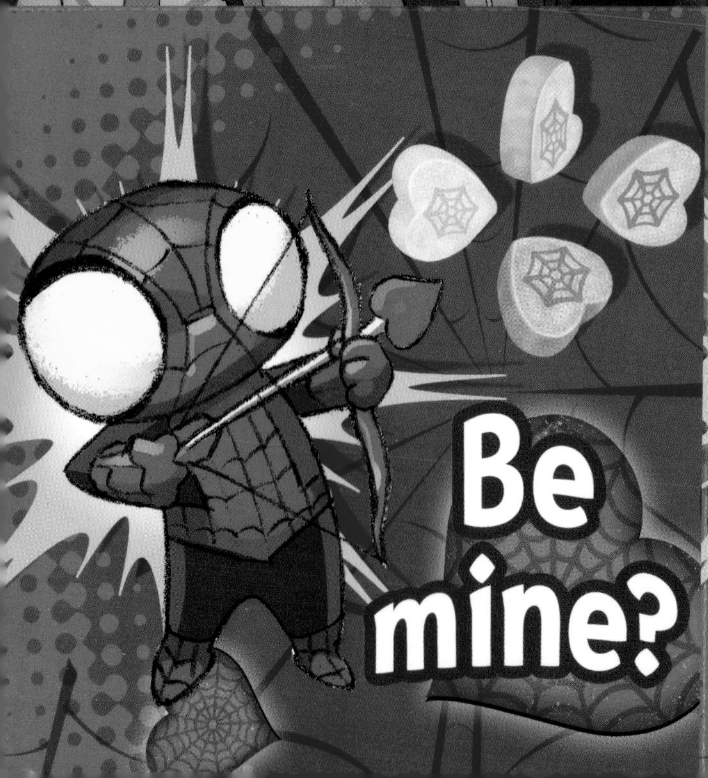
Be
mine?

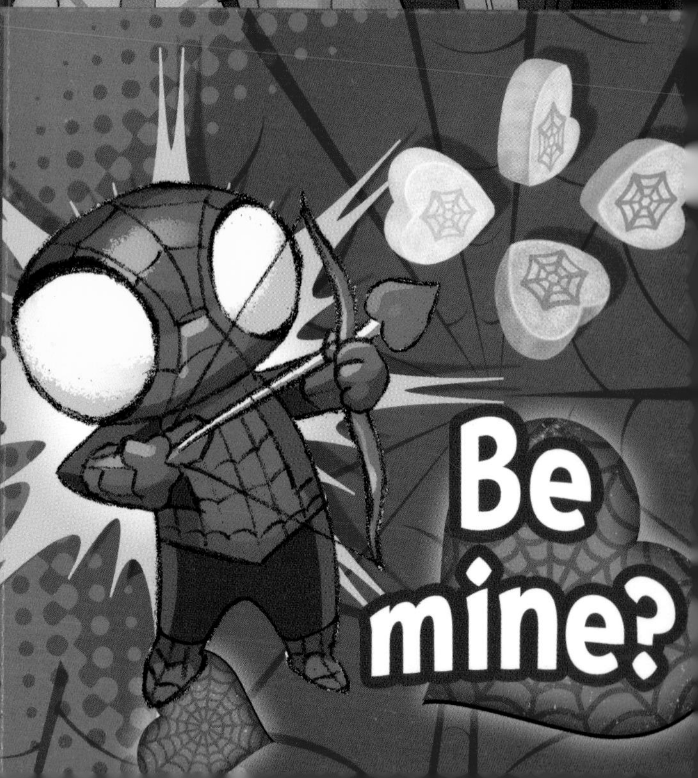
Be
mine?